Licensed exclusively to Top That Publishing Ltd
Tide Mill Way, Woodbridge, Suffolk, IP12 1AP, UK
www.topthatpublishing.com
Text copyright © 2015 Ellie Patterson
Illustrations copyright © 2015 Dubravka Kolanovic
All rights reserved
0 2 4 6 8 9 7 5 3 1
Manufactured in China

Written by Ellie Patterson
Illustrated by Dubravka Kolanovic

ISBN 978-1-78244-907-2

A catalogue record for this book is available from the British Library

Baby Bear

Written by Ellie Patterson

Illustrated by Dubravka Kolanovic

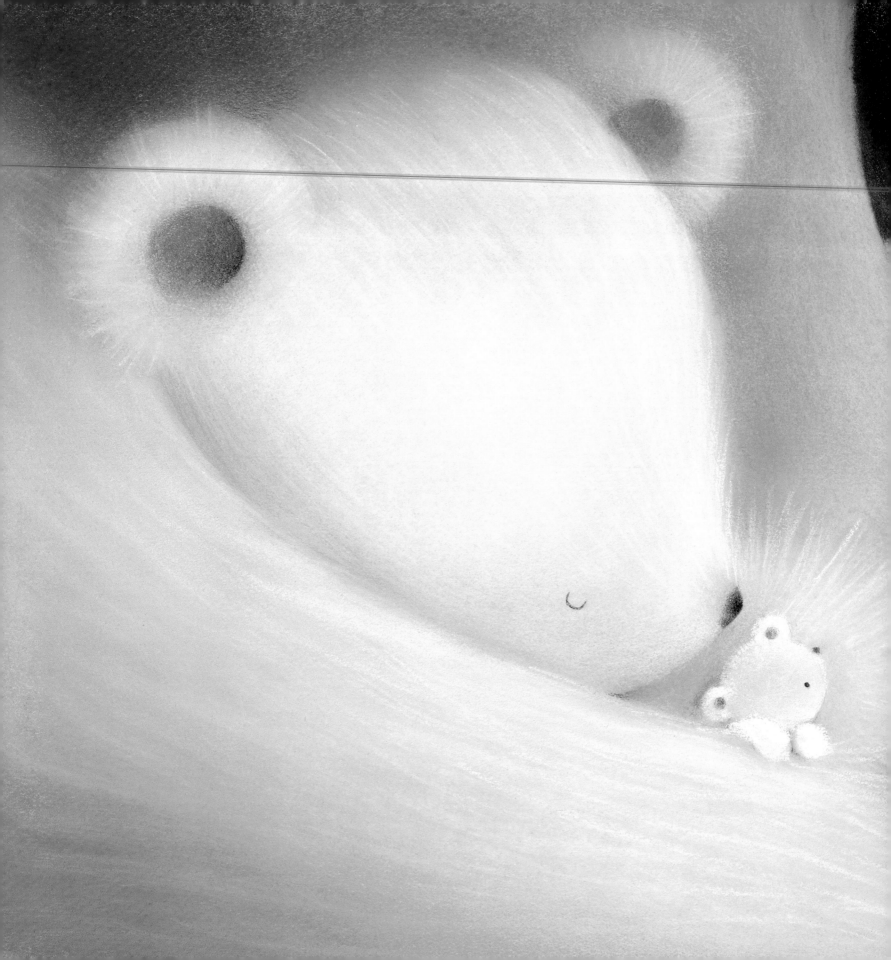

Inside his cosy den, Baby Bear was snugly and warm in Mummy Bear's arms. **Outside,** the big, wide world was cold and white.

No matter how hard he tried,
Baby Bear could not sleep.

He was curious.

Slipping out from Mummy Bear's arms,
Baby Bear peeped out at the
big, wide world.

It looked a little frightening, but he wanted to explore.

Stepping outside,
Baby Bear saw that there were footprints.

Big footprints.

Huge footprints!

A little **scared,**
he decided to follow them
to see where they led.

The big footprints went on and on,
winding down a path and through
deep, dark woods.

Baby Bear looked up
at the sky.
It was big
and dark
and beautiful.

Then he saw the moon,
and he thought that it looked like
a big hole in the dark night sky.

Suddenly, Baby Bear
began to feel very small
and very
      alone.

Soon, Baby Bear came to the ocean.
It was so big and so wide that just
looking at it made Baby Bear feel
even smaller.

Baby Bear sat down and began to wish that he
hadn't left Mummy Bear's snugly, warm arms.

Suddenly, there was a `Splash`, then there was a Sniffle, and then a small creature flopped onto the rock beside Baby Bear.

'Who are you?'
asked the small creature,
looking curiously at Baby Bear.

'I'm Baby Bear,' said Baby Bear.
'Who are you?'

'I'm Sammy Seal,' said Sammy Seal.

'Are you scared
of the big,
wide world too?'
asked Baby Bear,
realising that
Sammy Seal must
find it even
scarier than he did
because he was so small.

'Not really,' said Sammy Seal.
'In the ocean there are creatures that are
even smaller than me and they are not scared.
The big, wide world has lots of wonderful
things to explore, but you just have to be brave.'

'I'd like to be **brave!**'
said Baby Bear, hopefully.

'Well, why don't you come on a big adventure with me?' Sammy Seal suggested. 'I know lots of exciting things that we can do.'

'OK!' agreed Baby Bear, feeling brave all of a sudden.

From the top of a big iceberg in the middle of the big, blue ocean, Baby Bear and Sammy Seal watched whales *flipping and somersaulting* out of the water and named each of the stars in the sky.

Baby Bear began to feel very brave indeed sitting on top of the big iceberg with his new friend, Sammy Seal.

Soon, the big sun began
to rise over the big,
blue ocean.

The world was filled with
light and seemed like a warm
and welcoming place once more.
But it was time to go home.

So Baby Bear and Sammy Seal swam back to the shore.

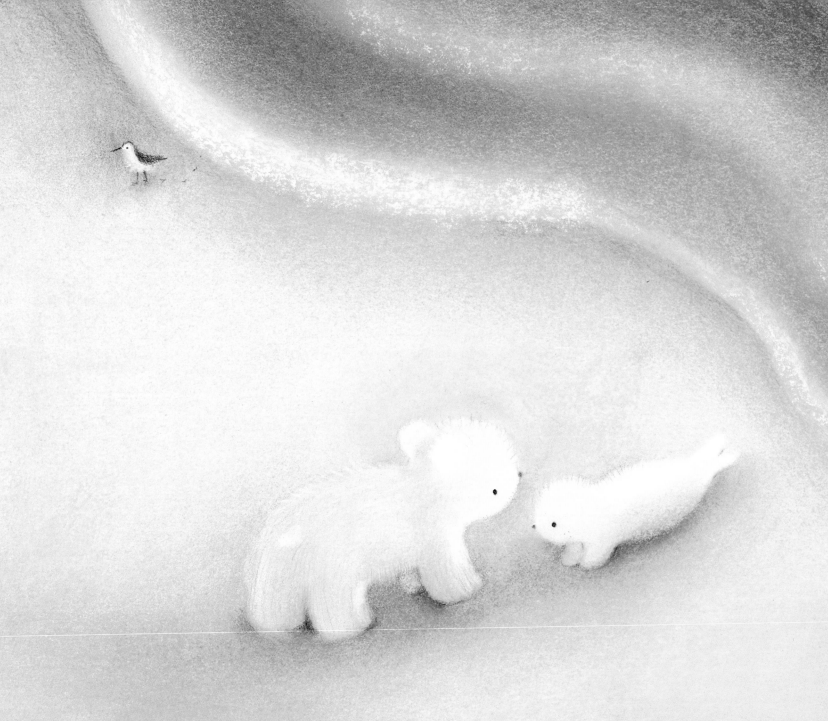

Baby Bear thanked Sammy Seal for showing him that the big, wide world wasn't as scary as he had first thought.

They agreed to meet up soon for another

big adventure.

Baby Bear followed the big footprints
all the way home.

He crept into Mummy Bear's
arms as quietly as he could
and fell soundly asleep.

Baby Bear had learnt that
the big, wide world is actually
not that scary ...

when you have a friend to
share it with.